Dear reader, welcome to Rusty's world in the North Amazon jungle. Sit on the branch of the giant kapok tree with him and see it through his eyes. Then make it yours too!

Also, please look in the back of the book for some Amazon facts and a glossary of words that are in bold in the text.

Happy reading!

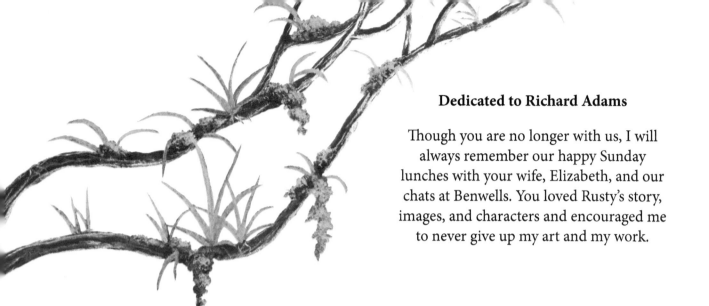

Dedicated to Richard Adams

Though you are no longer with us, I will always remember our happy Sunday lunches with your wife, Elizabeth, and our chats at Benwells. You loved Rusty's story, images, and characters and encouraged me to never give up my art and my work.

ISBN Hardcover 978-1-9168861-0-0

ISBN Paperback 978-1-9168861-1-7

Acknowledgements

Rusty Coati has been a labor of love, and it has finally come to life with the help of many friends whom I would like to thank:
Book design, Greg Morahan; I.T. support/consultant, Jean Marc Fernandez;
Photography (artwork), Andrew Robinson, Photofarm.co.uk;
P.R. support/consultant, Claudia Brooks D'Avanzo, www.creativecomminc.com.

A special thanks to Stuart Robinson for his editing insight and support through a friendship that was born and developed at the time of the *Watership Down* project.
Thank you to https://www.collinsdictionary.com/dictionary/english for helping us with our definitions.

THE RUSTY COATI SERIES - BOOK ONE
WWW.RUSTYCOATI.COM

RUSTY COATI

In Search of the Great River

Rusty popped his head out of the bush.

He looked around for Laelia. "Ha," he whispered. "She doesn't know where I am."

"See you," yelled Laelia. "You're it!"

"Oh no," Rusty groaned and hopped out of the bush. "Hey guys, want to dig for beetles—or we could race up the trees?!"

"No! You're it," shouted his good friend, Spotty, as the ring-tailed coatis scattered in all directions.

Rusty was about to close his eyes and start counting to ten when he suddenly stopped.

Next to a tree stood an odd-looking coati. He was the eldest of their kind and wore a large leaf around his shoulders. He also had a skull perched on his head from an animal none of them had ever seen.

Instead of continuing the game, Rusty decided they needed to find out what the strange coati had to say.

"Come on, Rusty," Spotty **scoffed**. "You can't take him seriously. Look at that thing he's wearing."

Rusty didn't pay any attention and called out, "Old Boris! What are you doing here?"

The **grizzled** creature grinned. Then stepping on a large root and pausing for a moment, he began: "It is time for you **younglings** to learn about this amazing place in which we live!"

Boris spoke about their giant kapok tree, towering above the **canopy**. "It was here long before the coatis came to this place and will be here long after we're gone."

He told the group of the many animals, insects, and smaller plants that live on the tree's branches. "The nectar of the flowers feeds the bats at night, and the bats pollinate the flowers, ensuring the tree brings forth its abundant fruit."

"The wind carries away the fruit's fluffy seeds. The rains fall and the cycle of life completes when **saplings** grow strong in the earth."

"You see? Every creature, every plant, the wind and the rain: all are connected in *our* jungle! Without them, your carefree life would not be the same."

"And far beyond this valley," Boris bored holes
into Rusty's eyes, "lie wonders you cannot imagine. Legend says there is a Great River—
a river so wide it cuts the world in two!"

Rusty was fascinated by the tale, but the others were less impressed.
Laelia giggled, and Spotty rolled his eyes.

11

"Shh," Rusty **chided** his friends. "He's trying to tell us something important!"

The young coati turned back around to speak to Boris but gasped, "He's gone!"

This made Rusty sad, so he sneaked off to his favorite place at the top of the giant kapok tree. He realized that the **wizened** coati had planted a seed in his mind.

Spotty quietly climbed up beside his friend. "Why did you leave?"

Rusty was gazing over the endless jungle that lay in front of him. "What if Boris is right? What if there is a whole wide world beyond what we can see? *What if* there is a Great River that cuts the world in two?"

Spotty rolled his eyes again. "It's just a story. And everybody knows **ole** Boris has lost his marbles!"

"Don't be rude," Rusty said. "I believe him! He says our lives depend on the **rainforest,** which is all wrapped up in that one river. I want to know if that's true, and there's only one way to find out."

Rusty sat up straight. "Spotty, I'm ready for an adventure! Want to go with me?"

Spotty scrunched his brows together. "Not me. No way! It'll be scary— and dangerous. Have you gone mad? We're safe here. There are a lot of predators in that jungle that would love to eat me *and* you."

Rusty stuck his tongue out, "Thhhhwwwwrrrp."

He raced down the kapok tree and bid farewell to his family and friends. He looked back for a moment at everything he was leaving and then headed into the unknown.

After walking for miles, Rusty's stomach began to grumble. He raised his long nose and took a whiff. "Umm. I smell ripening fruit."

The coati sped toward the mouthwatering aroma and found a family of collared peccaries gobbling up the fallen fruit from an ubos tree.

"May I share with you?" Rusty asked. "I'm mighty hungry."

"Sure," replied the biggest peccary, "but there's not a lot on the jungle floor."

Rusty knew just what to do.

He shot up the tree and shook the branches vigorously. Tons of fruit rained down over the **squadron**.

"Wow," one of the little peccaries grunted with joy, "now there's plenty for everyone!"

A little later, Rusty rubbed his full belly. "That's better! Thank you for letting me have dinner with you. I want to find the Great River. Do you know where it is?"

"Can't say we do," commented one of the large peccaries, his nose to the ground.

"Monkeys live in the canopy," another member of the family mumbled, chewing the last of her food. "They might have seen the river from up there. We know some monkeys. We'll take you to them, if you like."

"Yes, please," Rusty said. He climbed on the back of the largest peccary and off they all trotted through the **scarce** undergrowth on the dark forest floor.

They travelled for over two days. Rusty had not realized how immense the Amazon jungle really was, and he was grateful that his new friends were so helpful.

At last, the group spotted a squirrel monkey hanging upside down.

What could these crazy monkeys know, Rusty thought. Wait—I need to mind my manners and be friendly.

So instead he said to the peccaries, "Look! We've found them! Thank you for taking me this far."

"You're welcome," the big peccary winked as Rusty climbed off his back. "Good luck finding your river."

Rusty darted up the tree and turned to wave goodbye to the peccaries.

Then he looked at all the monkeys and wondered which one he should talk to.

Rusty didn't have to wait long. "Hello," one of them said, extending his hand. "I'm José. Nice to meet you."

"Oh hello! I'm Rusty. It's nice to meet you too. I've come to ask if you've seen the Great River."

Immediately the trees came alive with peeps and chucks and loud sounds as the gang consulted each other. The coati waited **expectantly**.

When it got quiet, José shrugged his shoulders. "We haven't seen it, Rusty. I do remember, though, that one of our neighbors mentioned a big river once. He might know a little more."

"Come with me, so I can introduce you to my pal, Bertie."

José scurried along a twisted vine, and Rusty followed him to a nearby tree where a family of emperor tamarins lived.

"Hi there, José. Who's this?" Bertie asked.

Joy, his baby, looked a little scared at this new animal Daddy's friend had brought.

"Meet Rusty," José replied. "He wants to find the Great River. Didn't you say you overheard some macaws talking about it?"

"I did!" said the tamarin. "They would know where it is because they fly long distances in search of food."

"Hmm, we need to find those parrots," suggested Bertie. "In fact, we'll come with you. We'd love to see the river!"

José tilted his head. "Hey, I'll come too. I want to see that river!"

Rusty's face beamed. "That's great! Traveling is always more fun with friends."

The monkeys and the coati followed all sorts of different trails through the jungle. No matter how hard they searched, they couldn't find the macaws.

After a full day of **scrambling** through the branches of the thick canopy, they crossed over a flooded area. There they found two magnificent birds.

"Ah, company!" one of them squawked. "I'm Diego, and this here is Alfredo. Rrrraaah."

"Hi, I'm Rusty Coati. Do you know how to reach the Great River? We're looking for it."

"We sure do," Alfredo called. "Just follow us."

The parrots flapped their wings and flew across the swamp. Soon they were out of sight.

"**Cheeky** birds," Rusty snorted. "They know we can't fly."

"They fooled us," cried José.

"Never mind," Bertie chimed in. "It won't help us to be mad at them. I'm thirsty. Let's go down to the flooded ground."

The companions made their way to the dark water.

"Oh look," Rusty said. "There's a school of fish. They may know."

José leaned over the fallen tree trunk. "Excuse me, fish. Do you know where we can find the Great River?"

Baby Joy squealed as the fish swam to the surface of the water. They were all baring their teeth!

"We're not going to tell you," barked one of the red-bellied piranhas, "and we'll bite your noses off if you try to take a drink."

"That's not very nice," Rusty woofed, dashing back up the tree with the others.

José yelled over his shoulder, "Ya know, you don't have to eat *everything*!"

"Over there are some bromeliad (bro·mee·lee·ad) plants!" cried Bertie. "We can drink the rain water straight from the leaves."

With their thirst **quenched**, the four snuggled into the bromeliads for the night.

Early the next morning, Rusty and his mates set off again.

When they reached the edge of the flooded area, they saw two large creatures in the water.

"They've got long noses, even longer than mine!" Rusty blurted out.

The older tamarin laughed at the coati's delight. "Yes, they use their snouts like snorkels."

That's neat, Rusty thought, then called hello down to the Brazilian tapirs.

"Well hello. I'm Cily, and this is my baby Chloe," whistled the mama. "We're enjoying a bath and eating some camu camu berries."

"Yum." Rusty licked his lips and asked, "Do you know where the Great River is?"

Two noses waved "no" in the air. "We've never been to the Great River," Cily bubbled up through her mouth as she and Chloe dipped back into the pool and swam away.

Rusty lowered his eyes. He was frustrated. "Why hasn't anyone seen the river? Maybe this journey wasn't a good idea."

José patted Rusty's back, wanting to cheer him up. "You've come this far. We need to keep trying."

The coati shook his head. He wasn't sure what he wanted to do next.

All of a sudden, there was a rumble coming from high up in a nearby tree.

"Helloooo down there."

The little band looked up.

A strange creature munched on the large cecropia leaves. It moved so slowly, it had to be the slowest animal in the forest.

"Iiiii'm Droooop," **lumbered** the three-toed sloth. "You seem trouuubled. Can I helllllp?"

"If you would, please," Rusty politely asked. "We're looking for the Great River."

Droop loved to talk. Even though it took a while, the sloth gave the travelers some good tips about their surroundings.

Finally he got to *the river*. "Earrrrlier in the season, I saw the floooood waters come iiiinnn. The Great River is thaaaaat way," he pointed with his long, sharp claw.

"Oh, thank you!" Rusty couldn't quite believe that someone knew where to go!

"**Cheerio**!" they all called as they marched in the direction Droop had **indicated**.

Rusty told Bertie, "I've just learned how valuable sloths are. You know, I always thought they didn't do much. Droop's really smart!"

After a while, José, Bertie, and baby Joy stopped to take a nap on a branch.

Rusty decided to search for beetles.

He was getting ready to drop to the ground when he heard a crunching sound.

Rusty froze. The coati could smell the predator before he could see it and knew at once why Spotty didn't want to come along on this adventure.

A jaguar crept out of the bushes.

"Hello, young coati," he growled in a low silky voice.
"My name is Rongo. Are you lost?"

Rusty didn't answer, so the big cat purred, "Let's play a game.
Guess how many spots are on my fur. You can come down
here and count them."

Rongo had enormous claws and his teeth looked razor sharp.
Rusty shivered. He had never seen a jaguar.

Droop warned us about the Lord of the Jungle, Rusty realized. He
could certainly eat me in one mouthful! This game must be a trick.

"I'm not coming down!" the coati snarled.

"Then I'll have to come get you," Rongo roared, climbing up the branch Rusty was sitting on.

Rusty spun toward the tree trunk and jumped— and not an instant too soon!

The branch broke off, dragging the big cat down.
It bounced on the forest floor, hitting him in the face.
"Mrrriaaaaaaaaaaooo!" Rongo screeched in pain.

It was the scariest moment of his life, but Rusty had
to be brave. I'm so close, I can't fail now and become
that jaguar's dinner!

43

Rusty zoomed to the top of the tree in a flash!

When he stopped, his jaw dropped.

There it was…

the Great River!

"José! Bertie! Baby Joy!

You *have* to come see this!" he yelled over and over.

"What's all the ruckus about?" José jumped to his feet and woke the tamarins.

The **trio** jetted up the tree. Once they could see through the dense branches, the monkeys knew. It wasn't because they were in trouble....

"We did it!" Bertie chuckled.

"What a sight!" added José.

Baby Joy giggled and pointed to an enormous lizard-like beast swimming beneath them. They watched the reptile wave its long, scaly tail until it dived with a splash and **vanished**.

"That must have been the large **caiman** that Droop mentioned," said José.

"The head!" Rusty shrieked. "It looked like the skull Old Boris was wearing. He *has* been to the Great River!"

47

Rusty told the others what Boris had said, "The river acts like a giant drain, taking away most of the rain that falls across our world. If it didn't do that, the jungle would be a swamp, and we wouldn't have a home!"

"The Great River *really* is the beating heart of the forest."

It grew dark. The mates marveled at the rising full moon and its reflection, shimmering over the **inky** surface from one bank to the other. They all agreed it was the most beautiful thing they had ever seen.

Down below, the waters lapped peacefully against the shore. In the tropical night, the Great River was singing its lullaby to the four tired-but-happy travelers, sending them off to sleep.

The next morning, the explorers headed back to their individual parts of the forest.

All-too-soon, José found his **troop**, and Bertie with baby Joy rejoined their family.

They all bid their farewells, hoping they would meet again.

A few more days passed before Rusty heard the waterfall and smelled the familiar scents of his valley.

He was nearly home.

When he arrived, Rusty raced across the clearing where they always played.

"I'm back! Hey guys!"

They all came running. Laelia hugged her **wayfaring** friend while Spotty demanded, "We want to know everything!"

Rusty stood tall and proud. He had fun telling them about his **expedition**, his new friends, and all the animals he had met—including the fish that threatened to bite their noses off!

Then he paused and lowered his voice. "The scariest part was my encounter with a jaguar, Rongo. He would have eaten me for sure, but I got out of there fast. That's when I first saw the Great River."

Spotty's eyes grew big. "You mean it's real? The legend is true?"

A smile spread across Rusty's face. "It sure is. The Great River really does cut the world in two!"

The coati pals stared at him in admiration when Spotty suddenly **chirped** with respect, "Gee Rusty, you sound just like Old Boris!"

Almost a year later, Rusty sat in the giant kapok tree, gazing at the stars twinkling in the darkened sky. Spotty, again, squatted next to him.

"You know, Spotty, I'm grown up now. That means it's time."

Spotty looked surprised. "Time for what?"

Rusty's face lit up. "It's time for me to find a new home. That means— it's time for a new adventure!"

Stay tuned for "Rusty Two: Across the Great River." I can't wait, hehehehe!

Amazon Facts

The Amazon forest is the largest tropical rainforest in the world, and its vegetation helps maintain our planet, making carbon dioxide into plant food and releasing oxygen. It is also precious for its enormous biodiversity; thousands of different species of animals and plants live here. Many products made from its plants have become part of our daily lives, including medicines, rubber, and cocoa for making chocolate. The Amazon forest is also home to many indigenous people and their tribes.

The Amazon River, the **Great River** in the story, is the widest river in the world, reaching almost 7 miles (11 kilometers) at its widest point in the dry season but growing much wider during the wet season. It is approximately 4,000 miles in length (6,400 kilometers), competing closely with the River Nile for the longest river. The Great River travels east in the heart of the Amazon forest, starting in the Peruvian Andes and ending at the Atlantic Ocean. Collecting all the rain in a vast network of rivers and streams, it drains the largest area of land on the planet (the **Amazon Basin**), and releases the largest amount of fresh water into the ocean, more than any other river in the world.

Jungle language: all animals communicate with each other with many different sounds. Just like in the story, coatis snort, woof and grunt, and they also chirp but in slightly different ways depending on whether they are happy or angry. Monkeys can peep, chuck, twitter and call loudly to each other, peccaries grunt, macaws squawk and scream, piranhas bark, tapirs whistle, and baby sloths even squeak if they get separated from their mother. The mighty jaguars purr and hiss and, like the other big cats (lions, tigers, and leopards), roar.

Blue and yellow macaws are large members of the parrot family that are social and intelligent. Their strong, curved beak is ideal for crushing nuts and feeding on fruit. Alongside monkeys in the canopy and ground animals like the peccaries and the tapirs, they provide a vital action as seed dispersers for the trees of the forest (that's what animals that scatter the seeds are called).

Bromeliads (bro·mee·lee·ads) are plants that grow without soil on the branches of the trees. Rain is collected in the leaves and stored at the center of the plants. They act like miniature ponds in the canopy, where frogs and insects lay their eggs.

Camu camu bushes produce purplish-red berries, the size of large grapes. They grow along the riverside in the Amazon rainforest and attract wildlife. The berries are harvested by people in canoes.

Cecropia trees are fast growing and reach 50 feet (15 meters) in height. They have distinctively long, thin trunks and few branches. The large, divided leaves are the main food of three-toed sloths. The regular presence of fruit provides a constant food source for birds, fruit bats, monkeys, and other animals.

Collared peccaries have light markings around their neck area and sharp, straight tusks. They are social animals and live in groups of up to twenty, called squadrons. They resemble a pig, but don't belong to the same family. These animals trample the forest floor in search of food. Breaking up the soil helps new plants to grow.

Emperor tamarins are tiny monkeys that live in small groups. The males take care of the youngsters and carry them on their backs, allowing more feeding time for the mothers. These monkeys get their name from the German Emperor Wilhelm the Second, because the Emperor was famous for his long, white moustache.

Jaguars are the top predators in the Amazon, with an important role in maintaining the ecosystem of the forest, helping to control other animal populations. They move silently and their spotted coat disguises them in the light and shade of the forest floor, allowing them to sneak up on their prey.

Kapok trees are giants of the forest and can live up to 300 years. They grow up to 230 feet (70 meters) tall. The umbrella-shaped **crown** stands high above the canopy. The flowers open at night and produce a foul smell that attracts bats. When the ripe fruit bursts open, the seeds' silky fiber allows them to be easily carried on the wind and spread across vast areas.

Piranhas have a fearsome reputation, although they live in shoals to protect themselves from their own predators: birds, crocodiles, and river dolphins. They have a single row of large, sharp, triangular teeth in both jaws.

Ring-tailed coatis belong to the raccoon family. They live in groups of adult females and youngsters. Adult males live in their own territory. Coatis are excellent tree climbers, which helps them find fruit, and stay safe. The long nose (snout) is used to find grubs on the forest floor.

Squirrel monkeys live in large groups of forty or more in the forest canopy. Their long tails help them maintain their balance on the tree branches. Youngsters are looked after by their mothers.

Tapirs are large animals, up to 6.5 feet (2 meters) long. They use their long noses to reach the tender leaves and berries on bushes and to find fallen fruit on the ground. They love to spend time in and under the water, feeding on soft plants, cooling off, and hiding from predators. Their snouts act as snorkels when swimming. Babies have striped and spotted coats for **camouflage**.

 **Three-toed sloths** are tree-dwelling animals with slow and sluggish habits. They have long claws that allow them to hold tightly onto the branches of trees, and their shaggy fur turns greenish with algae, providing them with camouflage in the branches.

Ubos trees grow up to 40 feet (12 meters) and are also called "hog plums" in the tropics. They produce small plum-like fruit that is light orange in color. The fruit attracts wildlife, particularly tapirs and peccaries.

Glossary

Caiman is a large predatory reptile, similar to a crocodile, that lives near the water.

Camouflage is when animals use leaves, grasses, twigs, and the colors on their hides to hide themselves in the jungle.

Canopy is the lush upper zone of the forest. It is formed by the **plant crowns**, including the smaller plants and animals that live in it. There are three layers in the jungle (shown on page 14). The middle layer between the canopy and the forest floor, is called the understory. Many plants have larger leaves in this section to capture the light that filters through the canopy. In the lower part, we find shrubs and saplings and the larger animals of the forest. The bottom layer is the forest floor, where plant and animal matter collects and decomposes through the activity of fungi and bacteria. There is little light down there and only a few plants can grow. This is why Rusty and the peccaries move through the scarce undergrowth on the dark forest floor.

Cheeky is a British expression meaning that someone is being a little rude or disrespectful but in a charming way.

Cheerio is a British expression that means goodbye, farewell.

Chided means that someone is talking to you in an angry way because you've done something bad or foolish.

Chirped is when animals make a short, high-pitched sound.

Expectantly means getting excited because something important might happen.

Expedition is an organized journey that is made for a particular purpose.

Grizzled means someone's hair (or fur on an animal) has turned grey as a result of growing older.

Indicated points out where something is.

Inky means black, as dark as ink.

Lumbered means to move or act slowly.

Ole is an expression of old.

Plant crown is the top part of the tree, made up by its branches and foliage.

Quenched means to drink until you aren't thirsty anymore.

Rainforest: any forest with a high level of rainfall throughout the year. Tropical rainforests have a warm and wet climate, and are located just above or below the equator (the imaginary line that cuts the Earth in half).

Sapling is the name for a young tree.

Scarce is when there is not a lot of something.

Scoffed means that whomever is speaking is not being respectful and helpful.

Scrambling shows the group is using their hands and feet to move quickly over the rough and awkward branches of the canopy.

Squadron: a group of peccaries.

Trio: a group of three individuals.

Troop: a group of monkeys.

Vanished means to disappear suddenly or in a way that cannot be explained.

Wayfaring describes someone who has gone on a journey.

Wizened is someone who is old and wrinkled.

Youngling is a young person or animal.

About the author and illustrator

Aldo Galli was born in Lombardy, Italy, in 1966.

He graduated in Agricultural Sciences at the University of Milan.

Passionate about the natural world and a keen artist, he loves the wet on wet oil painting technique for his colorful illustrations.

A trip to the Amazon in 2012 has provided the inspiration for Rusty Coati and his adventures.

He previously worked with Richard Adams on the creation of the fortieth anniversary illustrated edition of *Watership Down*, printed across the world in different languages.